P9-DNW-185

For Mimi—a friend
forever
—R.P.G.

For A.B.: my long-sleeve
plaid flannel friend
—T.E.

Fancy Nancy: Pajama Day

Text copyright © 2009 by Jane O'Connor

Illustrations copyright © 2009 by Robin Preiss Glasser

All rights reserved. No part of this book may be used or reproduced in
any manner whatsoever without written permission except in the case of
brief quotations embodied in critical articles and reviews. Manufactured
and printed in China. For information address
HarperCollins Children's Books,
a division of HarperCollins Publishers,
10 East 53rd Street, New York, NY 10022.
www.harpercollinschildrens.com

ISBN 978-0-06-208085-1

10 11 12 13 14 LEO 10 9 8 7 6 5 4 3 2 1

Fancy NANCY Pajama Day

by Jane O'Connor

cover illustration by Robin Preiss Glasser

interior pencils by Ted Enik

color by Carolyn Bracken

HARPER

An Imprint of HarperCollinsPublishers

"Class, don't forget!"

Ms. Glass says.

"Tomorrow is . . ."

"Pajama Day!" we shout in unison.

(That's a fancy word

for all together.)

I plan to wear my new nightgown.

I must say, it is very elegant!

(Elegant is a fancy word

for fancy.)

Then the phone rings.

It is Bree.

She says, "I am going to wear

my pajamas with pink hearts

and polka dots.

Do you want to wear yours?

We can be twins!"

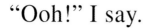

"Ooh!" I say.

"Being twins would be fun."

Then I look at my elegant nightgown.

What a dilemma!

(That's a fancy word for problem.)

Finally I make up my mind.

I tell Bree I am going to wear

my brand-new nightgown.

Bree understands.

She is my best friend.

She knows how much

I love being fancy.

The next morning at school,
we can't stop laughing.
Everyone's in pajamas,
even the principal.
He is carrying a teddy bear.

12

Ms. Glass has on a long nightshirt
and fuzzy slippers.
I am the only one
in a fancy nightgown.
That makes me unique!
(You say it like this: you-NEEK.)

"Nancy, look!" says Bree.

"Clara has on the same

pajamas as me."

Bree and Clara giggle.

"We're twins!" says Clara.

"And we didn't even plan it."

At story hour, Ms. Glass

has us spread out our blankets.

She reads a bedtime story.

Clara and Bree lie
next to each other.
"We're twins,"
Clara keeps saying.

At recess

Clara takes Bree's hand.

They run to the monkey bars.

"Come on, Nancy," Bree calls.

But it is hard to climb in
a long nightgown.
And I can't hang upside down.
Everyone would see
my underpants!

At lunch

I sit with Bree and Clara.

They both have grape rolls

in their lunch boxes.

"Isn't that funny, Nancy?"

asks Clara.

"We even have the same dessert."

I do not reply.

(That's a fancy word for answer.)

Pajama Day is not turning out

to be much fun.

I wanted to be fancy and unique.

Instead I feel excluded.

(That's fancy for left out.)

The afternoon is no better.

Clara and Bree are partners

in folk dancing.

Robert steps on my hem.

Some of the lace trim

on my nightgown rips.

At last the bell rings.

I am glad Pajama Day is over.

"Do you want to come
play at my house?"
I ask Bree.

But Bree can't come.

She's going to Clara's house!

I know it's immature.

(That's fancy for babyish.)

But I almost start to cry.

Then, as we are leaving,

Bree and Clara rush over.

"Nancy, can you come play too?"

Clara asks.

"Yes!" I say.

"I just have to go home first
to change."

Now we are triplets!

Fancy Nancy's Fancy Words

These are the fancy words in this book:

Dilemma—a problem

Elegant—fancy

Excluded—left out

Immature—babyish

Reply—answer

Unique—one of a kind (you say it like this:
you-NEEK)

Unison—all together